With special thanks to Conrad Mason

For Oscar and Casper Wood

ORCHARD BOOKS

First published in Great Britain in 2022 by Hodder & Stoughton

1 3 5 7 9 10 8 6 4 2

Text © Beast Quest Limited 2022
Cover and inside illustrations by Juan Calle
© Beast Quest Limited 2022
Illustration: Juan Calle (Liberum Donum). Cover colour: Santiago Calle.
Shading: Juan Calle and Luis Suarez

Series created by Beast Quest Limited, London

A CIP catalogue record for this book is available from the British Library.

ISBN 978 1 40836 800 8

Printed in Great Britain

FSC
www.fsc.org

MIX
Paper from
responsible sources
FSC® C104740

The paper and board used in this book are made from wood from responsible sources.

Orchard Books
An imprint of Hachette Children's Group
Part of Hodder & Stoughton
Carmelite House, 50 Victoria Embankment, London EC4Y 0DZ

An Hachette UK Company
www.hachette.co.uk
www.hachettechildrens.co.uk

SPACE WARS

COSMIC SPIDER ATTACK

ADAM BLADE

ORCHARD

Avantia ...

Once upon a time, it was a lush, green planet with sparkling blue oceans. A haven for life in all its forms, and a home to eight billion people. A place of incredible technology and culture.

Until the Void ...

In Avantia City, it struck on a clear day at the height of summer. No one saw it coming. No one understood it. And no one was prepared.

First there was a roar, like distant thunder. Then a swirling vortex ripped apart the sky, streaked with vivid green and purple storms of electricity. It was vast, like the mouth of a monster.

As earthquakes shook the ground, the citizens scrambled into any craft that could fly. They fled their homes, their very atmosphere ... and from the darkness of space, they watched the Void swallow their planet, leaving nothing behind.

For most, it was the end.

But for those lucky few, the survivors ...

It was only the beginning.

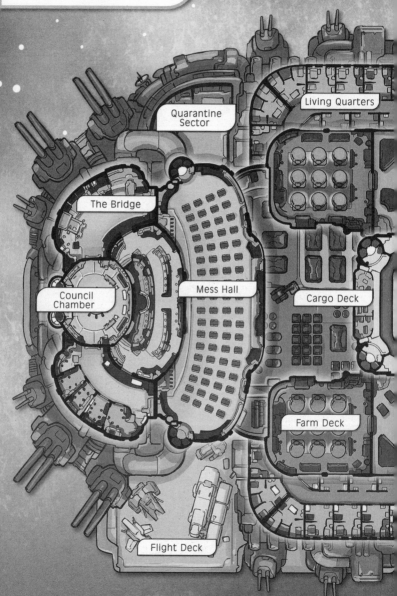

VANTIA 1
Plan

Quarantine Sector

Living Quarters

The Bridge

Council Chamber

Mess Hall

Cargo Deck

Farm Deck

Flight Deck

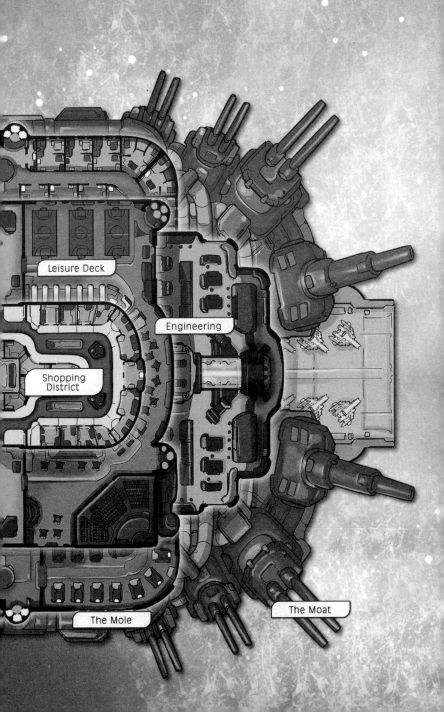

Leisure Deck

Engineering

Shopping District

The Mole

The Moat

1: *Harry Hugo* is a talented apprentice engineer, and there's nothing he can't fix.

2: *Ava Achebe* is a cadet, training to be one of Vantia1's elite space pilots.

3: *Zo Harkman*, Chief Engineer, has taken care of Harry ever since his parents disappeared.

4: *Markus Knox*, another cadet, *thinks* he's brave and daring …

5: *Governor Knox* is in charge of running Vantia1 and protecting all the station's inhabitants.

6: *Admiral Achebe* is the commander of the space fleet, and gives orders to the pilots.

CONTENTS

CHAPTER 1

EVASIVE ACTION

Energy bolts seared past Harry's flank. Gritting his teeth, he threw his Intercept, a small, speedy spacecraft, into a corkscrew roll over the planet's rocky surface.

CLANG! The Intercept rocked as an energy bolt glanced off its wing. Harry wiped sweat from his forehead. He twisted and slid beneath a rock archway. But when he glanced at his rear cam, his heart sank. The other ship was gaining on him.

He couldn't outrun it.

So I'll have to outsmart it.

Harry counted down in his head. *Three ... two ... one ...*

He slammed on the brakes, cutting all power to the engines. At the same time, he hit the take-off thrusters, boosting himself straight up into the air. G-forces pressed him into his seat. Below him, his pursuer streaked ahead. *Now who's chasing who?*

Harry focused, thumbs hovering over the red buttons. His heart pounded as

the target lock on his screen searched
for the enemy vessel. Any moment now
it would turn from red to green …

"End simulation," said a voice.

Everything went dark and silent. The
Intercept,
the rocky
valley, the
target …
They were
all gone.

Blinking,
Harry lifted
the SimSet
off his head.

He'd
almost

managed to forget where he really was
– in a simulator pod in the pilot training
bay in Vantia1. He felt a familiar pang of
disappointment.

There was a hiss as the top of the
pod lifted. Harry unclipped his belt and
heaved himself out.

"Now then. Thoughts? Comments?"

The speaker was a tall, serious-looking
man in a neatly pressed purple uniform.
Captain Nyman – leader of the cadet
force, and their teacher. His broad chest
glinted with gold braid. He had the
other cadets drawn up in ranks next to
the pods, watching a giant viewscreen
that had shown Harry's mission. Harry's
friend Ava had her arms folded, looking

distinctly unimpressed.

"Hopeless," snorted a blond-haired cadet in the front rank.

Harry rolled his eyes. *No surprise there.* It was Markus Knox, son of Governor Knox herself, and bane of Harry's life.

Nyman stopped, his eyes narrowed beneath his bushy grey-black eyebrows. "Explain, Cadet Knox."

"He was supposed to fly straight to the refuelling station." Markus sneered. "Robo-arm couldn't even follow one simple instruction."

Harry felt a flash of anger. *Robo-arm, cyborg, half-metal freak ...* he'd heard it all before, mostly from Markus. The robotic fingers of his prosthetic hand twitched, whirring faintly as they curled into a fist.

Captain Nyman raised a finger. "Now, that's not—"

"That other ship was toast," interrupted Harry. "Just a few more seconds and—"

"It was a *recon mission*, dummy," hooted Markus. "Not a dogfight! You were supposed to avoid detection. You're a disgrace to the cadets!"

"Enough!" Captain Nyman barely raised his voice, but it silenced every single cadet – even Markus. He peered around with his stern grey eyes, his gaze settling at last on Harry.

"Knox is correct, Cadet Hugo. Granted, this is only a training simulation. But what is the first rule of cadet training?"

An unenthusiastic chorus of voices rose from the cadets. "Always obey orders."

Out of the corner of his eye, Harry saw Markus smirking at him. "What does it matter anyway?" Harry couldn't stop himself now. "We'll never fly to a real planet, will we? We're stuck here on this floating tin can, probably for ever!"

There was silence throughout the bay, and everyone was looking at him. A hot flush crept across Harry's cheeks. He knew straight away that he'd gone too far.

Captain Nyman strode towards him, hands firmly clasped behind his back, expression severe. Harry steeled himself. *I'm in for it now …*

But when Nyman reached him, he just put a gentle hand on Harry's shoulder. As the captain leaned down, Harry saw something in his eyes that was even worse than anger.

Pity.

"You're excused, Cadet Hugo," said Nyman, quietly. "Take some time to calm down." He beckoned to Ava. "Cadet Achebe, go with him."

As the Captain turned away, Harry couldn't help but notice Markus guffawing with his friends. When he saw Harry looking, he rubbed at his eyes, pretending to cry.

Harry opened his mouth, ready to sling a parting line at Markus ... but Ava already had a firm hand on his shoulder, steering him towards the exit.

"So I have to ask," said Ava, as she led him to the nearest Mole. "Are you actually *trying* to get kicked out of the cadets?"

Harry shrugged. With his friend at his side, he could feel his anger leaking away, leaving behind a hollow feeling. "I don't care."

"Yeah, right," muttered Ava. "Harry Hugo doesn't want to be a pilot? Give me a break."

Harry sighed. She was right, as usual. Once, being a cadet had been all that he wanted. But that was before he had learned the truth about Vellis. About his parents.

They had reached the Mole now. The elevator system carried citizens all around Vantia1, the huge space station which served as a refuge for the people of Avantia. *My real home.* Avantia had been destroyed by one of Vellis's experiments – the deadly Void that he had created.

And my parents along with it ...

While they waited for a pod, Harry gazed out of a huge observation window that stretched from floor to ceiling. There was the darkness of space, filled with glittering stars. A ring of flashing glow-buoys that marked the edge of the

Exclusion Zone around the station. And beyond them, the Void itself. A vast, swirling vortex of crackling green light that seemed to watch,

taunting him, like a monstrous eye.

Leaning close to the glass, Harry could see the gleaming outer hull of Vantia1 falling away below the window. The TechDroids were hard at work once again, operating in clusters to repair the damage from Vellis's latest attack on the station. Most of the cargo deck was still closed off, chunks of the hull torn clean away.

Harry felt a shudder run through him at the thought of Vellis's deadly Gravity Squid, its dangling robotic arms reaching out to kill, smash and destroy ...

"Hey, are you OK?" asked Ava.

Harry blinked and looked at his friend, her brown eyes full of concern. He plastered on a smile as best he could. "I just know they're out there," he said at last, in a quiet voice. "Somewhere in the Void. They can't have died. They can't be just ... gone. Right?"

Ava nodded. "Right."

But Harry could tell that the smile she wore was every bit as fake as his own.

CHAPTER 2

PROJECT INTREPID

*"**Deck 2. Mess** Hall,"* said the smooth robotic voice of the Mole.

The pod cruised to a halt, the doors slid open and Harry and Ava stepped out into the canteen. Luckily it wasn't too busy right now. Most of the engineering staff were still working double time to repair the space station.

"Cheeseburger and fries, please," said Harry, as they reached the counter. A robot arm swivelled out and dumped a collection of slimy brown cubes on to Harry's plate.

"Nice try," said Ava, grinning.

Harry sighed. *Food biomes are still out of action, then.* It had been long-life nutrient algae blocks for longer than he cared to remember. Only six, too.

"I swear it gave me ten at breakfast."

"Rationing," said Ava, collecting a little pile of cubes on her own plate. "Until things are back to normal."

They sat at a table in the corner. Harry tried to pretend the food was delicious, but its stale, mouldy flavour really wasn't helping.

"Has your mum mentioned anything about Bremmer lately?" he asked.

Ava looked up sharply. Bremmer had been Governor Knox's secretary, until he'd betrayed the whole space station and fled into the Void to join his master, Vellis. Worse, Bremmer had stolen a special suit that enabled the wearer to travel into and out of the Void. It had been designed by Harry's guardian, Zo Harkman.

Ava shrugged and pushed a cube around her plate. "Mum doesn't tell me much. I've barely seen her in weeks."

Harry nodded. It was no wonder

Admiral Achebe was busy, working hard to restore the station's defensive systems.

"Hey, it won't be for long," he said, trying to cheer Ava up. "Zo's the same right now. Working all hours."

"It's not that." Ava frowned, then glanced around and lowered her voice. "You know, there was one thing ..." She leaned across the table, lowering her voice. "The other day, Mum left a file up on the holoscreen in our quarters. I didn't see much, but she couldn't shut it down fast enough. I checked afterwards. The file was locked, obviously. But it was called ... *Project Intrepid*. Mean something to you?"

Harry shook his head. "Could be anything." He clenched his fists with frustration. He hated being kept in the dark – especially now, when Vellis had the power to leave the Void. When he could attack at any moment …

"Well, this has been … disgusting," said Ava, pushing away her plate and standing up. "I've got to hit the Shopping District. Mum's birthday is coming up, and I need a present. Not that she'll be taking time off for it."

As soon as Ava was gone, Harry took the Mole straight down to Engineering. He picked his way carefully across the enormous hangar, weaving in between

busted star-choppers, skipping over wires and dodging sparking automatic phase welders. The sounds of laughter, whirring machinery and clanging hammers rang in his ears.

"Hey there, Hazza," called Mei, who was dressed in overalls, her face smeared with oil. She waved a spanner cheerfully at him. "Slumming it down here again?"

Harry smiled uncomfortably. He'd once been a grease monkey, just like her, until his promotion to Cadet. "Just picking up some antimatter convertors," he shouted back. "The old Space Stallion's nearly up and running."

"You're wasted in the cadets," snorted Mei.

"We got a couple," said her buddy, a big tattooed man called Jackson. He rested his boot on a pair of metal convertors beside their work station. "What are they worth to you?"

Harry dug in his pockets. "I've got fifty Leisure Deck credits," he said, pulling out some plastic chips. "Wait ... fifty-five."

Jackson jutted out his chin, unimpressed. "Well. Since you're a buddy."

"I owe you," said Harry, handing over the credits and tucking the convertors under his robotic arm.

"Whoa, not so fast," said Mei, as Harry turned to leave. "First, tell us, what's the scoop on the Cargo Deck?"

Harry blinked. "What do you mean? I know it's being repaired, but—"

"Nuh-uh," said Jackson. "Something else going on."

"We've been shipping tech down there for a week," said Mei. "Serious tech."

"Security's tight, too," added Jackson.

34

"Harkman's been down there a lot, so I heard."

"Really?" said Harry.

"I guess it's above your pay grade." Mei gave him a wink.

Harry was frowning as he carried the convertors back to the Mole.

Project Intrepid … the Admiral's secrecy … now a mystery on the Cargo Deck.

What on Avantia are they up to?

Back in his room, Harry got to work with his screwdriver finger appendage, fitting the antimatter convertors to his Space Stallion.

It had taken hours of painstaking work

to restore his bike after the damage it had suffered in the fight with the Gravity Squid. But now, finally, every dent was knocked out of it, the chrome was polished up and the red paint gleamed. The convertors were the final touch.

"Done," muttered Harry, as he thumbed the ID pad.

"Long time no see, partner," said the Space Stallion, as it hummed into life. Its thrusters lifted it off the floor.

"I missed you, buddy," Harry told the bike.

"Don't go gettin' soft on me, partner."

Harry chuckled. He went to the door, checking that Zo Harkman still wasn't back. *All clear* …

"A.D.U.R.O.?" he asked.

The station's AI unit appeared before him, an ageless female face with smooth skin and a shock of spiky white hair. "Good afternoon, Cadet 34002."

"Access file," Harry commanded. "Project Intrepid."

"Denied. File classified," said A.D.U.R.O. Then she vanished immediately.

Harry slumped on his bed, feeling disappointed, but not surprised. *No way it was going to be that easy to figure out.*

From the next room he heard the smooth sliding sound of the doors opening.

Leaping up, he went into the main

living space to find Zo Harkman hanging up his lab coat. Harry's guardian had bags under his eyes, and his hair stuck up in all directions, making him look both exhausted and strangely startled.

"Busy shift?" asked Harry.

"You don't want to know," said Zo, wearily.

I really do, thought Harry. He put on the most innocent face he could manage. "Hey, settle a bet?"

Zo grunted as he popped a can of energy drink and settled himself on the couch.

"Mei says there's something weird happening on Deck 10. I told her she was nuts. She's nuts, right?"

Only someone who knew Zo as well as Harry did would have noticed Zo's flinch, just before he got control of his expression. "Droids are fixing it up, that's all," he said. "Don't listen to gossip, Harry."

Zo was lying. No question.

"That's what I thought," said Harry.

He hesitated. "I was only wondering if it had anything to do with that material you invented, for sending things into the Void?"

A cloud crossed Harkman's face, and he set the can down on the coffee table so hard it spilled. "Harry! We've talked about this a hundred times."

"But imagine if we really could go into the Void …" Harry felt hope bubbling up inside him. "Who knows what's in there? Who knows what survived when Avantia was swallowed?"

Harkman had a sad look in his eyes. Clearly he knew exactly *who* they were talking about. "I'm sorry, Harry," he said, more gently. "The suit wasn't ready when

Secretary Bremmer stole it. He could easily have died in the Void – or worse. It was a foolish idea in the first place."

He ruffled Harry's hair as he headed for his room. "Next shift's in three hours, so I'm going to get some kip. Keep the noise down, all right?"

"Sure," said Harry.

He wasn't going to stick around anyway, because now he was more certain than ever. *There really is something secret happening on the Cargo Deck.*

CHAPTER 3

THE SHELL

Harry passed a queue for the one Mole port that was actually working on deck and kept going. Around a corner he found what he was looking for. A disused Mole shaft, the doors closed and plastered with yellow and black tape. A sign read "Out of Order".

Perfect.

He shot a glance over his shoulder, but there was no one around.

Quickly Harry ripped off the tape. He extended an electronic jack from his robotic arm and slid it between the doors. Maxing out the synth muscles, he strained at the door. It squealed in complaint, but slowly shuddered open. He slipped through the gap.

There was no pod beyond the doors – just the Mole shaft extending upwards and downwards, a metal tunnel with offshoots leading in all directions.

Five decks down to Cargo. Luckily, there was a maintenance ladder. Harry gripped it with his prosthetic hand, letting it take his weight, then rested his boots either side of the rungs. Loosening his grip, he slid downwards.

One deck ... two decks ... He lowered himself down and down, further into the abyss. He could hear the swish of distant Mole pods, but thankfully he didn't meet any. His neck was prickling with sweat by the time he reached Deck 10.

The doors of the disused port on the Cargo Deck were already half open. Harry squeezed through. He found himself in an empty corridor, but in the distance he could hear noises. Voices, the clanging of hammers, the *beeps* of diagnostics and the *fizz* of phase welders. He followed the sounds, creeping as quietly as he could. Whatever was going on down here, Harry knew one thing for sure – he wasn't authorised to see it.

The corridor led out on to a viewing platform that overlooked the main Cargo Deck. Harry dropped to his hands and knees as he peered through the railings.

His breath caught in his throat.

Far below, he saw a large battle cruiser bristling with energy cannons. Technicians swarmed across the ship, checking weapon housing, testing landing gears and adjusting phase ports.

"Ready!" called a chief technician from below. "Bring us the shell."

Harry narrowed his eyes as he saw four technicians wheeling a trolley across the deck. A silver case sat on top. Everyone had stopped work to watch as the trolley squeaked closer to the battle cruiser.

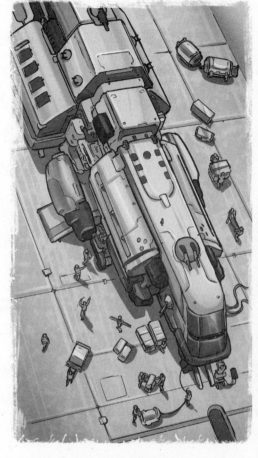

What was *the shell*?

The chief tech hopped down from the cruiser hull and went to open the case.

Harry frowned. Inside were three silver orbs on a red cushioned lining. Each one was no larger than a Zero-G handball. The chief tech rolled up her sleeves and slowly, carefully, lifted one out.

Harry watched as the woman carried the orb to a hatch on the underside of the craft's hull. She held it in place as two other techs adjusted connections and closed off the hatch.

"Stand back!" called the chief tech. Everyone scrambled off the ship, retreating to behind a yellow line that ran all around the vessel. "And … activate!"

A low hum filled the whole deck, and a murmur rose up from everyone watching. Harry gasped in astonishment.

A silvery force field was shimmering

into life all around the hull of the battle cruiser. It was translucent, its surface shifting and changing like the rainbow patterns on an oil slick. It was beautiful …

The murmur turned to applause, then a chorus of whoops and cheers.

And suddenly Harry understood. *The shell!* It was a force field, but no ordinary one. It must be the same technology that Zo had used to build his special suit – the one that Bremmer stole. The technology that protected against the effects of the Void.

I know where this ship is going … thought Harry, hardly daring to believe it.

CHAPTER 4

DEEP SLEEP

"Are you serious?" Ava said the next morning. "A force field for a whole ship? To go into the Void?"

"Deadly serious," said Harry.

They were talking in low voices beside the lockers on the Training Deck. Cadets milled around, waiting for Captain

Nyman to arrive. Harry had hardly slept for thinking about his adventure on the Cargo Deck.

"Project Intrepid …" murmured Ava. "No wonder Mum's been keeping it secret."

"Right. And if they're going into the Void, you know what that means …"

Ava nodded slowly. "They're going after Vellis!"

"What I wouldn't give to be on that ship …"

"Harry." Ava laid a hand on his arm, and Harry was surprised to see concern written all over her face. "I know you think …" She caught herself. "I mean, I know it's possible your parents might be out there, in the Void. But you're not going to do anything stupid, are you?"

Harry bit his lip. *Define stupid*, he wanted to say. He didn't want to lie to her, that was for sure.

Luckily, he didn't have to.

"Hey, can opener!" Markus came swaggering over, with a couple of his friends

in tow. "You going to blow a fuse again today?"

Ava moved between them and seemed about to speak when the door slid open and Captain Nyman strode in. Harry and Ava scrambled to form ranks along with the other cadets.

Captain Nyman was frowning even more severely than usual, and Harry's skin prickled. *Something's up ...*

"Today's classes are cancelled," said Nyman. Harry blinked, and a murmur rose up from the cadets. Nyman continued over the noise. "This morning we have received an urgent directive from the High Council of the Post Planetary Authorities." Harry noticed Ava raise her eyebrows. The High Council consisted of the governors from every one of the nine space stations where the survivors of Avantia lived. "In light of ongoing food production issues, Vantia1 is to be temporarily evacuated. Only essential personnel will remain on board. Transports leave today."

Some cheered, while others groaned. Harry and Ava exchanged a shocked glance.

"Even cadets?" asked Ava.

"Indeed, Cadet Achebe." Captain Nyman held up a finger for silence. "Only military and select engineering personnel will be staying. Everyone else is bound for Vantia2. It's four weeks' space flight away, and I suggest you get packing." He clicked his heels and executed a salute. "Cadets ... dismissed!"

Excited conversations broke out as the cadets shuffled to the exit.

"My cousin's on Vantia2," someone was saying. "She says they've got a waterpark!"

"I've heard they've got eight Zero-G chambers," someone else said. "And no algae blocks for breakfast!"

All Harry could think about was the battle cruiser down on the Cargo Deck. *Project Intrepid*. It couldn't be a coincidence that they were evacuating the station now, just as the ship was ready to launch.

"I've never been to another station," muttered Ava.

"Me neither," replied Harry grimly. *And I don't plan to now.*

"This isn't a choice, Harry," said Zo Harkman. "You're going!"

Harry glanced around their quarters and saw no sign of packing in the living space. "But *you* get to stay?" he said.

Zo rubbed his temples. "I'm Chief of Engineering, Harry."

"So I'm out on my own, then?"

"Captain Nyman will keep an eye on you, and on Ava Achebe too. I've already spoken to him."

"I—"

"The arrangements are made. The High Council's decision is final."

Harry's chest felt tight. He hesitated, wondering how far he dared push his guardian. "So this has got nothing to do with … I don't know, *Project Intrepid*?"

Zo leapt off the couch as though he'd been stung by a warp worm. "This again!" His face was red – with anger or embarrassment, Harry couldn't tell. "What have you heard?"

Harry hesitated. But with Zo in this mood, there was no way he was going to mention his little adventure on the Cargo Deck. He shrugged. "Enough."

Zo nodded. "Well, that makes two of us. Get packing. Now."

It took Harry ten minutes to throw
what few belongings he had into a bag.
He looked round his little bedroom,
wondering when he'd next see it.

"So long, partner." He patted his
deactivated Space Stallion. Then, with
a sigh, he shouldered his bag. Zo called
goodbye to him from the couch as he
left, but Harry couldn't bring himself to
respond.

Ava was waiting in the corridor
outside, her own kitbag at her feet.
Together they took the Mole to the
Flight Deck, joining the crowds swarming
around vast transport ships. There were
hundreds of people – almost all the

inhabitants of Vantia1, gathered together on one deck.

"Who are they?" asked Ava. She pointed over the heads of the crowd.

Standing on his tiptoes, Harry saw a dozen black-clad troops marching off the ramp of a small military vessel, phase rifles shouldered.

"Marines?" said Harry.

But what are they doing here?

Before he could see any more, he and Ava were carried onwards by the tide of people. They were in the shadow of a transport vessel now, and heading for the boarding steps.

Harry clenched his fists. *We're running out of options.* Any moment now, he and

Ava would be on board, and it would be goodbye to Vantia1. Goodbye to Project Intrepid.

Goodbye to any hope of seeing my parents again ...

At the base of the steps, a security guard was scanning everyone's ID. "Hugo, Harry," he said. "Pod 182C."

It was like a beehive inside, rows of identical life-pods extending as far as he could see, stacked five high. Each pod glowed with a soft blue light.

"Looks like we're neighbours," said Ava, tapping a button to release the lid of her own pod – 183C.

Harry followed suit. As the lid hissed open, he saw that the blue glow came from a kind of soft jelly that filled the inside of the pod. "Gross," he muttered.

"It's only for a few weeks," shrugged Ava, climbing into the jelly in her pod. "And you'll be asleep, anyway."

Harry winced as he lowered himself in and felt the jelly pressing coldly against his body. Where it touched his skin, it felt strangely dry. He'd never been in a life-pod before, but Zo had told him all about them. They put the user into a deep sleep for long journeys through space.

Four weeks ... thought Harry. *Who knows what will have happened by then?* The battle cruiser would be long gone. Would Zo be on board it? Admiral Achebe?

He felt his frustration mounting again.

"Ava?" he called. "Can you hear me?"

But there was no reply, just another soft hiss as the lid of his pod closed.

"Prepare for deep sleep," said a calm voice from speakers somewhere in the pod. "In three ... two ... one ..."

CHAPTER 5

STOWAWAYS

"Rise and shine ..."

Harry woke to the gentle words of the automated voice. He blinked in the soft blue glow of the interior.

Already?

The smooth white pod door lifted to reveal Ava's face grinning down at him.

She was scraping blue jelly from her uniform.

"That was the quickest four weeks ever," Harry said.

"That's because it was less than two minutes," said Ava.

"Huh?"

"We're still on Vantia1. I had to wait till everyone else was asleep." She threw an arm round, indicating the other life-pods. Harry saw that they were all full of sleeping passengers. "I had to disable my pod, obviously, so it wouldn't send me to sleep too." She held up the power cable of her pod – unplugged. "It wasn't exactly rocket science. Now come on, before the ship takes off!"

Together they crept along the rows of closed pods, their footsteps clanging and echoing on the metal deck.

Harry shivered. It was strangely eerie on board, with everyone else unconscious. But excitement was surging through him. If they could just get off this transport, there was still a chance that he could somehow board that battle cruiser …

"There." Ava pointed to a narrow hatch at the end of the aisle, with pod cables running through it. She frowned. "Too small to get through, though."

"Leave it to me."

Kneeling by the hatch, Harry tapped at the miniature control panel embedded in

 his robotic forearm. With a quiet whirring sound, a laser cutter extended from his knuckles. He activated it, and a lethally hot red beam burned into the metal around the hatch, melting and warping it. At last, Harry was able to bend it back with a good kick of his boot.

"Nice!" said Ava.

Peering through the hatch, Harry saw a tunnel descending into darkness. "Where do you think it leads?"

Before Ava could reply, there was a soft rumbling under his feet.

Engines firing up …

"No idea," said Ava. "But we'd better find out."

Quickly, Harry lowered himself into the dark tunnel below, followed by Ava.

The metal walls of the chute were vibrating as the ship's thrusters stirred. They were slippery too, and Harry scrabbled for purchase with his boots. He began to feel himself sliding downwards.

Nothing else for it. Lifting his feet, Harry let himself go.

He slid faster, hurtling down the chute until there was no hope of stopping himself. He closed his eyes tightly. Any moment now …

Ouch! Pain jarred through his back as he landed hard on something. He rolled aside just in time before Ava came thumping down beside him. She groaned softly.

The rumbling had risen to a roar, so loud it hurt Harry's ears. Smoke filled his nostrils and he blinked, eyes watering. Then he punched the air. *Yes!*

They were on the Flight Deck, the whole hangar filling with smoke as the transport vessels prepared for take-off. Harry grabbed Ava by the arm and pulled her to her feet. They ran across the deck, half stumbling, and threw themselves down behind a large stack of cargo crates.

Harry watched the vast bulks of the transport vessels taxiing slowly through the airlocks, each one carrying a full load of Vantians. "There they go …" he muttered, as each drifted out into space.

Finally there was silence all across the Flight Deck. Harry and Ava were alone.

Stowaways … thought Harry. *In our own home.*

"Thank you," he said, quietly. "If you hadn't busted us out, we'd be on our way to Vantia2 right now."

"No problem," Ava said. "I'm not that into waterparks, to be honest. So, what now?"

"We find out exactly what Zo and your mum are up to." Harry pointed upwards. "We've got to get to the Bridge."

"Without being seen," said Ava, raising an eyebrow.

"What are you like with confined spaces?" asked Harry.

"Are we there yet?" whispered Ava.

"Almost." Harry squirmed the last metre to the grille and moved aside so that Ava could squeeze in next to him.

They'd been crawling through the service ducts for what felt like an hour. The cramped conduits were barely big enough to crouch inside, and Harry's elbows and knees ached.

Ava wiped sweat from her forehead. "I'm never going to complain about waiting for a Mole again."

Peering through the metal bars, Harry saw that they had arrived just where they'd planned. They were looking out of a ventilation unit across the main Observation Deck, otherwise known as the Bridge. The sight of it still took his breath away. It was a huge transparent dome at the very top of the station, thirty metres across. The bustling brain of Vantia1, from which the whole station could be controlled.

As usual the Ob Techs were hard at work at their consoles, monitoring sensors and speaking into headsets.

Governor Knox sat in the command chair on the main platform, overseeing the Bridge. With her calm and quiet authority, it was hard to believe that she was from the same *species* as Markus, let alone that she was his mother.

Zo Harkman stood at the governor's side, muttering to her. And hovering at her other shoulder was the metre-tall holographic face of A.D.U.R.O., listening impassively to the chief engineer.

"Where's my mum?" whispered Ava.

Harry frowned. "I can't see her."

Then Governor Knox spoke up. "Patch us through to the *Intrepid*."

An Ob Tech tapped at a console, and a rectangular portion of the dome turned into a screen showing Admiral Achebe's face. She was wearing a flight suit and strapped into a crash seat. "Ready to launch, Governor," she said. "Omega Squad are all on board."

She's on a ship, Harry realised. The *Intrepid* – surely that had to be the ship he had seen on the Cargo Deck? *Project Intrepid*. And Omega Squad – could that be the troop of marines they had seen arriving on the Flight Deck? It was all coming together now.

He felt a pang of frustration. If the Intrepid was about to launch, he had missed his chance to get on board.

"We'll see you on the other side, Admiral," said Governor Knox.

Achebe gave a curt nod, and the screen disappeared, leaving only the view beyond the dome – countless stars twinkling in the darkness of space.

"*Intrepid* is go, Governor," said an Ob Tech.

Ava let out a soft gasp as they saw the *Intrepid* streaking out from somewhere below, its engines leaving fiery blue trails as it hurtled away from the station. Harry noticed his friend's fingers tightening on the bars of the grille as they watched. *She must be worried sick.*

"It's too soon," said a gruff voice. It was Zo Harkman, frowning hard at the sight of the ship. "We should have run more tests."

"Noted," said Governor Knox coolly. She clicked her fingers at an Ob Tech. "Keep monitoring the shell. Any hint of a problem, we'll call them back at once."

Harry shot a glance at Ava and saw her eyes widen with anxiety.

"It will be fine," he whispered. "I'm sure of it." But his own stomach was squirming with nerves. He had seen what happened with Zo's early experiments: the plants he had sent into the Void had come back looking like liquefied spinach.

"Entering the Exclusion Zone," said Achebe over the intercom.

"Give us a visual," ordered Knox.

A screen appeared once again, showing a view from the cockpit of the

Intrepid. Harry saw the flashing lights of the buoys that marked the edge of the Exclusion Zone. And beyond, the

sight that never failed to fill him with awe, and fear – the whirling green-gold vortex that haunted his nightmares …

The Void.

It seemed close – horrifyingly so. And the *Intrepid* was heading straight for it.

"Stand by," said Admiral Achebe. Was that the faintest tremble in her voice? *She's afraid*, thought Harry. *It would be crazy not to be.*

The Void was looming, filling the whole screen now. The ship was bound straight for the darkness at its heart, where crackles of electrical storms danced, flashes of unearthly light that made the whole Bridge glow.

"Touching the Void," said the Admiral. "In three … two … one …"

The screen died. Nothing but blackness.

Harry's heart stopped as gasps rang out around the Bridge.

"What's happening?" squeaked Ava.

Harry didn't know what to say.

"Locate the *Intrepid*," barked the Governor. Even she was leaning forward in her command chair.

"Scanning …" said A.D.U.R.O., calm as ever. "The *Intrepid* cannot be found."

Ava let out a whimper.

"Open a comms channel," said Zo grimly.

"On it," said an Ob Tech. "Nothing yet."

Silence had fallen across the Bridge. A minute passed. Then another.

"Anything?" said Governor Knox.

Harry felt Ava sag against him. He held her tighter, tears pricking at his own eyes. *It can't be*, he told himself. *She can't just be gone. Not Admiral Achebe.*

"Attention, Observation Deck," said Governor Knox, getting up. She was paler than ever, swaying slightly as she stood. "Understand one thing. None of you are to blame for this. I bear full responsibility for this mission. You have all—"

A voice interrupted her.

"Vantia1? Come in, Vantia1. This is Admiral Achebe. We've made it. We're here. We're *inside* the Void."

Gasps and cries of relief rose up all around. Harry could hardly believe what he'd just heard.

"She's all right," whispered Ava. "She's alive." She hugged him, and they clung to each other in shock and relief.

"Admiral ..." said Governor Knox, when

the hubbub had died down at last. "You don't know how glad I am to hear your voice. Report – what can you see?"

"Not much," said Achebe. "Space dust is obscuring our visual sensors, but ..." She trailed off.

"But what?" asked Zo Harkman.

"Oh my ... It's ... it's a planet."

There was silence once again. Harry could hardly breathe. He knew everyone was thinking the same thing that ran through his own mind, over and over.

A planet. Could it be ...? Is there any way ...?

"Visuals incoming," said A.D.U.R.O., with not the slightest trace of excitement. Her eyes flashed white, and an image beamed on to the screen from the cockpit of the *Intrepid*.

Harry stared.

It *was* a planet. No blue-green paradise, though. It looked rocky, grey and red and ravaged by swirling storms. A wasteland. Doubt flickered through his mind for just an instant.

"Is that what I think it is?" said Governor Knox quietly.

"Computing planetary size and gravity strength ..." said A.D.U.R.O. "Complete. Planet can be identified with 98.2% accuracy. Planet is Avantia."

"No ..." breathed Ava. "No way."

Harry felt dizzy. Was this really happening?

"We're scanning for signs of life," said the Admiral. "If all looks good, we'll—"

As she broke off, Harry heard other voices over the transmission, talking urgently to Achebe. His pulse quickened.

"What's going on?" Governor Knox demanded, a note of panic in her voice.

"Shields up," barked Achebe, and Harry realised she wasn't talking to Vantia1 any more. Whatever was happening had pulled her attention right back to her ship.

"Admiral, report!" snapped Knox.

Instead, the image of Avantia flickered and died.

"Visual contact with the *Intrepid* is lost," said A.D.U.R.O.

But they could still hear the voices from the cockpit.

"Bring the cannons online," Achebe was commanding.

"What the … ?"

"What *is* that?"

The transmission dissolved into static. Only a few disjointed words escaped.

"Don't …"

"… approaching … it's …"

"… looks like a … Spider …

"I can't …"

A crashing, rending sound jolted Harry's heart. Ava let out a cry of shock. Someone was screaming on the *Intrepid*. Screaming and screaming and then …

Nothing. The transmission was dead.

CHAPTER 6

NANOOK

The Bridge was in chaos.

Everyone was shouting, running between the consoles and trying desperately to make contact with the *Intrepid*.

"A rescue mission," Zo was saying. "It's the only way to—"

"No," Governor Knox cut him off. "We don't know what's out there. I'll not risk losing more good people."

"What happened?" whispered Ava to Harry. "What *was* that?" Her eyes were wide, her expression set in a grim frown of sheer disbelief.

"I don't know," said Harry. "But I think … I think something must have attacked them." *Spider.* The word was seared into his mind. But what kind of spider could take on a battle cruiser? Unless it had something to do with Vellis. Another deadly creation …

"Those were marines on that ship." Ava looked at Harry, with pleading in her eyes. "They're the best soldiers in the galaxy. They would have fought it off, wouldn't they? Whatever *it* was."

"Right," said Harry. But he could see that Ava didn't believe it – not really. *And I don't, either.*

"Come on," he said, putting a hand on her shoulder. "We're not leaving your mum out there. We're going to figure out a way to save her."

Harry followed Ava into the main living space of her quarters on Deck 5. It felt good to be out of the hot, cramped ventilation shafts but his mind was boiling with anxiety, and he couldn't imagine how much worse it must be for Ava. He winced as he saw her stop dead, staring at a holoscreen projection image of herself in cadet uniform, her mum standing proudly by her side.

"First day of cadet training," she said quietly.

Harry didn't know what to say. "I … I'm so sorry," he mumbled.

Ava flashed him a fierce look. "She's not *dead*," she snapped. "She can't be."

Harry nodded dumbly. All he could think of was telling Ava the same thing about his own parents, lost in the Void. *Are we both just lying to ourselves?*

Ava began pacing the room. "They've got to send a rescue mission, right?"

"Knox was dead against it," said Harry, as gently as he could. *I'll not risk losing more good people*, she had said.

But perhaps it wasn't her risk to take.

Harry bit his lip. "There might be a way for us to get into the Void ourselves."

Ava's eyes widened. "Spit it out."

"If we could just—"

"Harry?"

They both froze at the voice. Harry whirled around, but there was no one in the room with them.

"Answer me, Harry." It was Zo's voice, he realised, coming over the station's intercom system.

Ava put a finger to her lips. Harry nodded.

He can't know where I am, he realised, *or I would already have been arrested*.

"I know you and Miss Achebe are on the station," said Zo. "We've had a communication from the *Exodus 2*. Your pods were found empty on a routine scan."

Harry could hear his guardian trying to remain calm. "You're not in any trouble. I just need to know that you're safe."

Harry's heart sank. Zo really *did* sound upset. Admiral Achebe was his friend, and he was probably just as worried about her as Harry was. Now he had this to add to his plate.

Maybe I should answer …

A glance at Ava brought Harry back to his senses. If they told Zo where they were, they would be picked up right away. There'd be no hope of getting out into the Void. No hope of saving Ava's mum.

"Last chance, Harry," said Zo. "Don't be foolish."

Harry crossed to the sofa, took Ava by the hand and pulled her to her feet. She looked startled as he led her out of the quarters into the corridor. *No mics here – we should be safe.*

"What are we doing?" asked Ava.

"What's it look like?" Harry smiled as he saw the hope kindle again in her eyes. "We're being foolish."

Once they were settled in the saddle, with Harry at the handlebars and Ava behind, he thumbed the ID pad.

The Space Stallion purred to life. Its monitor glowed blue, LEDs flashing across the control panel. Slowly, the thrusters lifted them up into the air.

"Hold on tight, amigos," said the robotic voice.

"You bet," said Harry, twisting the throttle. The Stallion

jolted forward, engines roaring. Ava gasped.

"Woohoo!" whooped Harry as they shot down the corridor. He leaned into a corner, steering for the service ramps. He swooped and swerved, driving the Stallion down in a spiral as they descended towards the Cargo Deck.

"I've warned you, Harry." The voice of Zo over the station intercom echoed in the metallic confines of the service ramps. "A.D.U.R.O. is scanning for you now."

"Come on … come on …" Ava muttered.

Harry revved, driving the Stallion as fast as it would go.

One last turn and they came shooting out on to the Cargo Deck. Harry swung the handlebars, braking as they skidded to a halt, his stomach lurching as it was left behind. He heard Ava panting behind him.

He was just about to dismount when a holographic projection half the height of the deck sprang into life in front of them. It was an image of A.D.U.R.O.'s head.

"Cadet Hugo located on Deck 10. Cadet Achebe located on Deck 10," said the AI.

No ...

"Harry!" There was a dangerous edge to Zo's voice now. "You had better not be doing what I think you're doing."

Casting desperately around, Harry spotted the trolley he had seen before, with the silver case. "Hang on," he told Ava. He twisted the throttle again. They burst through A.D.U.R.O.'s image, roaring over to the trolley.

"Security is on its way," Zo warned. "For the love of Avantia, just ... *please*, give yourself up."

"Harry," said Ava, uneasily. "Are you sure you're ... OK with all this?"

He glanced over his shoulder and saw doubt in her eyes. But there was none in his own mind. Leaning over, he lifted the lid of the case to reveal the two remaining silver orbs, nestled in their red velvet lining. Up close, he saw that they weren't orbs at all, but polyhedrons with hundreds of flat sides. He took one, marvelling at how light it was, and tucked it into the Stallion's side compartment.

"Now all we need is a ship," said Harry. But his heart sank as he looked around. Most of the deck had been cleared in preparation for Project Intrepid.

"How about that one?" said Ava, pointing at a vessel.

Harry groaned. It was an old lumbering model with a peeling paint job – a Nanook class freight craft. Huge and hulking and *very* slow. It dwarfed them, so big it nearly scraped the ceiling.

But it was a ship, and its boarding ramp was already lowered.

"It'll do," said Harry.

He spun the Stallion around. Then a shout came from behind.

"Security! Freeze!"

Harry didn't even look back. He gunned the engine, racing across the Cargo Deck and up the ramp.

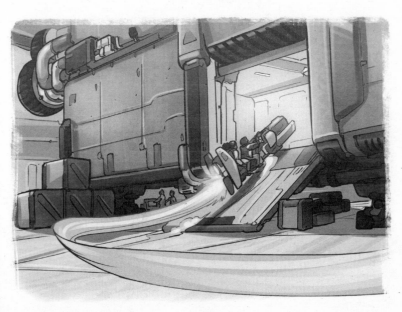

Blaster bolts singed and sizzled through the air. One glanced off the Nanook's hull with a metallic *clang*. Harry knew the blasters would be set to "stun", but they would still hurt like crazy at best – or at worst, knock them unconscious.

At the top of the ramp, Harry hit the brakes and they threw themselves off the Stallion. The interior of the Nanook was dark and cavernous, piled high with crates on all sides.

Ava scrambled to hit the green button that raised the ramp. With a series of beeps and a squeal of metal, it slowly began to lift. Harry could see the squad of security guards through the narrowing gap. They broke into a run, boots pounding the deck as they charged.

Time to get out of here!

Harry darted for the cockpit, dodging crates. Ava vaulted a barrel and overtook him, flinging herself into the creaky, beaten-up old pilot's seat. Harry took the navigator's seat next to it.

A chugging, roaring sound filled their ears as Ava engaged the engines.

"Step on it!" Harry yelled, as the Nanook began to jolt forward.

"What do you *think* I'm doing?!"

They were jerking forward in fits and starts.

"That way," said Harry, pointing to an airlock.

Slowly but surely, the Nanook was

building speed. *Clink*s and *clang*s rang out as the blaster bolts peppered its hull. *It might be slow, but at least it's tough!*

"Here goes nothing," shouted Ava. She slammed her palm on to the

launch button.

The engine rumbled to an unbearable pitch as they hurtled straight for the airlock.

There was a flare of light across the viewscreen as they crackled through the force field.

Then they were out and powering through the vastness of space.

7

HOME

Ava activated cruise mode, and the engines' roar died to a quiet shudder.

"Changing course," she muttered, adjusting the steering unit.

They both stared in silence as the Void appeared across the viewscreen. Was it Harry's imagination, or were the crackles of green lightning and electrical storms swirling more violently than usual? *Like it just can't wait to swallow us up …*

He pushed the thought from his mind.

Clambering over the back of the navigator's seat, he made his way through the cargo hold to where he'd left the Space Stallion, propped up against a pile of crates. He took the rounded silver gadget from its side compartment and turned it over in his hands, inspecting it.

"Just got to figure out how it works," he remarked.

"You mean … you don't know?"

Harry ran his fingers over a narrow groove running around the orb's equator. He tried pulling it apart, then pushing it together. Nothing happened. Then he twisted the two halves in opposite directions.

Click.

The silver ball gave off a soft humming sound.

"Whoa," gasped Ava from the cockpit.

Harry saw that a shimmer had appeared across the viewscreen. Now it seemed as though they were looking at the Void from inside a bubble, its surface shifting with rainbow colours. It was the same shield he had seen covering the *Intrepid*, back on Vantia1.

Yes!

He tucked the shell-generating orb

back into the Stallion's compartment and hurried to the cockpit.

"Entering the Exclusion Zone," said Ava. The quaver in her voice was unmistakeable.

Harry's stomach was flipping with anxiety. He'd been so sure of his plan. But now they were really here, their faces bathed in the eerie light of the Void, he was starting to have second thoughts. *What if we don't make it?*

Either way, it was too late to back out.

"My head ..." muttered Ava.

Harry could feel it too – a pressure building inside his skull. His whole body was tingling, as though it could sense the presence of the Void. "I don't ... feel so good," he croaked.

Ava was shaking, her eyes bulging as they came closer and closer.

The terrible eye of the Void had them in its grip now, and Harry couldn't help but stare into that horrifying darkness at the heart of it.

What have we done?

And then there was a thundering in his ears, and the light became blinding, driving out everything from inside his skull: all thoughts, all feelings, all consciousness and …

Blackness.

Harry swam in it, weightless. Silence enveloped him.

He felt dizzy and nauseous. But definitely alive.

He opened his eyes. And all the breath left him.

Avantia.

There it was, filling the viewscreen. It was so much larger, so much more real than the image they had seen on the Observation Deck. Its grey surface was pitted and scarred, with red clouds swirling across its atmosphere.

"We did it." Ava's voice brought him back to the cockpit. She was staring at him. "We're inside the Void."

"I can't believe it." Harry's voice was a croak. He looked down at his hands, flexed his fingers. Everything was …

normal. The cockpit was just as it had been a moment earlier. "I'm OK," he said. "Are you?"

Ava nodded. "I think so. Except … whoa!" Her eyes went wide.

"What's wrong?"

"It's your face, Harry. It's … it's turned green!"

Worry spiked through Harry's gut. "What do you mean? Is there a mirror? I …" Then he saw Ava shaking with silent laughter. "Oh. Very funny."

"You have no idea," said Ava, wiping her eyes. She settled at last, turning serious. "So, what now? I can't see the *Intrepid* anywhere. Maybe they crash-landed on Avantia?"

Harry turned to the controls, tapping buttons to bring up the sensor array. "There's something nearby," he said, frowning. "It's closing on us."

"Can we get a visual?"

"Not with this heap of junk," snorted Harry. "But if you steer us starboard …"

Ava adjusted the steering unit and, slowly, something began to appear at the corner of the viewscreen.

Harry's blood froze in his veins.

"What is *that*?" whispered Ava.

One word ran through Harry's mind. Almost the very last word they had heard spoken from the *Intrepid*.

"Spider," he breathed.

It was vast, almost as big as the

Nanook, with a segmented metal body and many eyes that glowed red like hot coals. Eight jointed legs probed and sliced through the darkness, each tipped with razor-sharp metal points. Harry knew at once it was another of Vellis's terrible creations.

And it was heading right for them.

"What on ..." gasped Ava.

The robotic spider splayed its legs and curled its abdomen underneath itself. Then a gout of ice-blue webbing sprayed from a tube at its rear. Its legs worked like knitting needles, picking up the webbing and launching it towards the Nanook.

"Take evasive action!" called Ava.

Harry could almost have laughed. *This ship couldn't evade a space slug, let alone a giant robot monster!*

There was a crash, and the hull shuddered, forcing Harry to grip his armrests tightly.

"It's on us!" yelped Ava.

CLANG!

Harry flinched as a massive dent appeared in the top of the cockpit, the metal crushed by the impact of one of the spider's pointed legs.

Blue strands sprayed across the screen, obscuring their view of Avantia.

"It's wrapping us in its web," said Harry. He checked for defence mechanisms, but the Nanook had

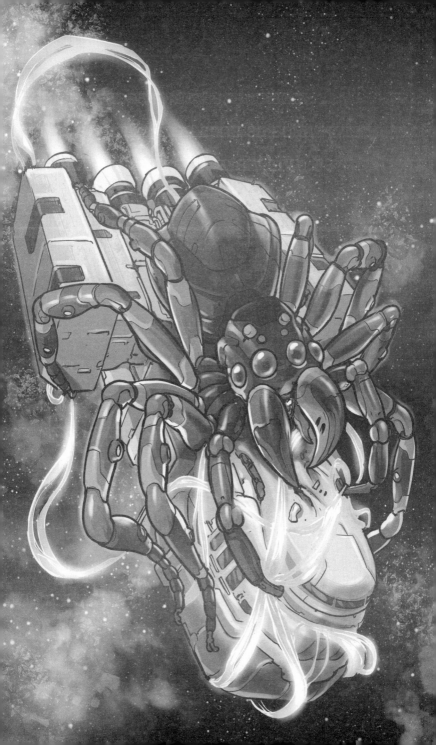

nothing. Not a single cannon.

There was a groan of metal, and Harry felt the hull listing as they were pulled off course, moving steadily away from Avantia. An alarm began to wail from the cargo hold behind them.

"Hull integrity failing," said Ava, checking the controls. "Systems scrambled." She looked at Harry, eyes wide with fear. "Where's it taking us?"

"I don't want to find out!" said Harry.

He leapt from his seat and ran across the hold to the Space Stallion, stumbling halfway as the spider slammed another pointed leg into the Nanook's hull. "Come on!" he shouted as he climbed on. "We're out of here!"

"One minute." Ava tapped furiously at the controls. Then the ship's automated voice spoke. *Self-destruct in thirty seconds. Twenty-nine … Twenty-eight …*

"Nice work," said Harry, as Ava ran and climbed on to the back of the Space Stallion behind him. "Activate skins."

They hit the buttons on their belts and their transparent space-skins spread over their clothes, encasing their heads in bubble-like helmets.

Harry fired up his Space Stallion. "Giddy up, partner," he muttered.

Harry armed the Stallion's rocket launchers. With a smooth hum and a click, they locked into place on either side. "Go time."

Whoooosh! The rockets launched in twin clouds of smoke. *BOOM!*

Harry winced, blinded by light as the explosions tore through the hull. As the smoke cleared he saw a ragged hole in the side of the ship, framed by twisted metal, with empty space beyond it.

"Go!" yelled Ava.

Harry twisted the throttle.

The Stallion leapt forward, shooting out into space at top speed.

The infinite darkness engulfed them, and for a moment Harry was overwhelmed by vertigo. Turning in his saddle, he saw Ava looking back too.

A cold knot of fear settled in his stomach, as he saw the spider crouched on their ship. The hull was entangled in its pale blue web. The spider's legs dug into the metal, crushing the Nanook slowly, like it was a tin can.

"Any ... moment ... now ..." murmured Ava.

A fiery cloud billowed out from the ship, sending warped bits of metal shooting through space. *The self-destruct.* Clouds of smoke drifted, shrouding the scene.

Did we destroy the spider?

"Let's not hang around," said Ava, tapping him on the shoulder.

Harry nodded, then brought the Stallion round to face Avantia.

I'm going home.

CHAPTER 8

INTRUDERS

Harry had fantasised about this moment so many times, but the reality wasn't quite what he'd imagined.

Instead of clear blue seas and lush green vegetation, they were hurtling towards swirling black clouds that half veiled the grey, rocky terrain below.

"Any sign of the spider?" he called over his shoulder.

"Nothing." Ava's voice was crystal clear through the space skins' intercom system. "I think we destroyed it."

"Entering atmosphere now," said the Space Stallion. "Trail's about to get bumpy, amigos." Almost at once, Harry was jolted in his saddle. He ducked down low and clung on tight to the handlebars.

"Hold on," he told Ava.

They swooped down through a bank of cloud, so thick that for a few moments Harry could see nothing but darkness. A roaring began to sound in his ears, and a vicious wind tossed the Stallion around. Harry routed more power to its thrusters to compensate.

As they dropped below the clouds, the stormy winds died quickly. Then Harry saw what lay below, and his stomach dropped away.

A city, utterly ruined.

It lay half buried in dunes of rocky rubble, and only the tallest buildings emerged. Their highest levels were battered or entirely broken, the bridges and walkways between them collapsed. A hyper-rail ran here and there, its plexiglass chutes cracked, staved in or gone entirely. The rest was all buried. Yet still there was something he recognised from his history lessons at school.

He pulled up the Stallion, letting it hover in the air.

"Is that … Errinel?" Ava's voice was hollow with shock.

Harry could only nod. *The greatest city on Avantia.*

"I was born here," he said quietly.

He felt Ava's hand gently resting on his shoulder. *There's no time for this. Not yet*. He gathered himself. "Come on. We have to find your mum."

"Can this thing scan for life forms?" asked Ava.

"This *thing*'s got feelings, ma'am," said the Stallion. "Scanning now … Twenty miles east. Thirteen humans."

"They're alive …" breathed Ava.

Harry's heart leapt. It had to be the crew of the *Intrepid*.

He took one last look back at the ghostly ruin of Errinel. Then he gunned the engine and they tore off through the sky.

They banked, flying high over a clutch of mountains that rose to jagged points. They dived low over a vast forest that stretched as far as the horizon. The trees were huge but bare – malformed and twisted things with grey branches, each one like a bony skeleton writhing in pain.

"There!" yelled Ava, pointing over Harry's shoulder.

Peering closer, Harry saw a massive scar carved into the forest, where trees had been uprooted, crushed and flattened, as though by some huge object. And sure enough, at the end of the scar, where it had finally skidded to a halt at the bottom of a wooded valley, was a broken spaceship.

Harry recognised the battle cruiser immediately. The *Intrepid* looked battered and damaged, but it was all in one piece. With a shift of the handlebars, they dived, coming down fast. On reaching the ground, Harry powered down the Stallion and dismounted, leaving it resting beside the wrecked ship. Up close, he could see massive dents and gouges in its hull, where the robotic spider had attacked with its deadly legs.

"Air looks good," said Ava, checking a wrist monitor.

They disengaged their space skins, and Harry drew in a deep breath. He couldn't help smiling. *Fresh air ...* The first he'd breathed since he was a little kid.

A smell of burning and smoke lingered in the air, though from the looks of it any fires on board the *Intrepid* had been put out.

So where are the crew?

"Harry."

He turned to see Ava looking at him, wide-eyed with shock, pointing at his chest.

Looking down, Harry felt a jolt of fear. A red laser dot was hovering right above his heart. As he watched, a second joined it, then a third.

He glanced up to see another two red dots dancing on Ava's uniform.

Slowly, carefully, he raised his hands and placed them on his head. Ava did the same. "We're not here to hurt anyone!" Harry called into the forest.

A woman stepped silently from behind a tree.

"Then don't move a muscle," she barked.

It took Harry a moment to recognise her, with the black and grey camouflage paint streaking her face. It was one of the marines he had seen on the Flight Deck. She had grey combat plates strapped on over her black uniform, and she was levelling her phase rifle straight at him. The laser sight winked red.

Out of the corner of his eye, Harry saw more movements among the trees. Several other members of Omega Squad were emerging from their hiding places, each one pointing a phase rifle at them.

One of the marines was talking into a headset. "Admiral. We've got intruders."

"That's my *mum* you're talking to," said Ava. "And we're not *intruders*. We're here to rescue you."

Harry thought he saw the marine's mouth twitch, holding back a smile. "Two kids, come to rescue a full squad of marines?"

Harry felt his cheeks heating up. He was about to snap back a retort when a service port on the *Intrepid* slid open, and a familiar figure dropped to the ground and landed in a crouch.

"At ease!" ordered Admiral Achebe.

"Mum!" Ava flew across the ground and flung herself into her mother's embrace.

Harry's heart lifted. All around, he could see the marines slowly lowering their rifles.

But a moment later the Admiral stepped back, holding Ava at arm's length. She looked as if she had suddenly remembered herself, and her face was stormy. She turned her glare on Harry, pinning him to the spot. "What are you two doing here?"

Ava's jaw fell open. Then her brow creased into a frown too. "We're getting you out of this mess, that's what we're doing!"

"You can't be serious." Admiral Achebe rolled her eyes. "*How* are you going to save us? Our engines are offline. That … *thing* busted the fuel cells."

One of the marines jerked his rifle at the Space Stallion, grinning unpleasantly. "Reckon they're gonna fly us all out on this space donkey, ma'am?"

The other soldiers chuckled.

"Admiral?" said Harry, carefully. "Could

I maybe take a look at those fuel cells?"

Admiral Achebe's glare became somehow even more forbidding. But Ava stepped up to Harry's side and laid a hand on his shoulder. "Harry's an engineer, Mum – remember?"

"Fine," growled Admiral Achebe. She waved a hand at the ship. "Captain Tex, keep an eye on him."

A broad-chested marine stepped forward. He had a short dark beard, a buzz cut and a scattering of stars tattooed across his thick neck. "On me," he grunted.

Harry followed, hurrying to keep up with the big man's long strides.

They climbed an access ramp on to

the ship. It was dark inside, with only a few strips of soft blue emergency lighting to help them see where they were going. Harry flinched as an electrical spark crackled from a severed cable. *That spider really did a number on them ...*

"In there," said Captain Tex, pointing down a hatch.

Harry slid through into the engine room, slung on the underside of the hull. He sucked air through his teeth at the sight of the fuel conduits. Fine cracks had spread across them. One was completely smashed. The fuel cells flickered with an uncertain red glow.

"Report," said Captain Tex. Harry got

the sense that the man didn't talk any more than he had to.

"It's not good," Harry admitted. "But I might be able to re-route. We could get back some thruster power, maybe fifty per cent."

"That enough?"

Harry nodded. "I think we can clear the planet's gravity."

Captain Tex didn't reply, just gestured at the fuel cells with his phase rifle. Harry figured the conversation was over.

CHAPTER 9

A FAMILY REUNION

Harry's screwdriver whirred as he fitted the final screw back into the fuel cell casing.

At last he retracted the tool into his forearm. He didn't know how long it had taken, but it felt like hours. He was hot and covered in sweat and grease.

"All done?" asked Ava, peering down through the hatch.

"Reckon so."

She reached through the hatch and he took her hand. She heaved him up on to the deck.

The sun had set, and the sky was a deep twilight blue.

Admiral Achebe was waiting for them on the ground, with Captain Tex at her side.

"I've patched up the cells," said Harry. "Isolated the ones that are still functional. With any luck—"

Suddenly Admiral Achebe's communicator crackled into life. "Incoming. Take cover."

Captain Tex grabbed Harry's shoulder with a massive, heavy hand and hauled him and Ava down behind a nearby bush. The Admiral took cover beside them.

Harry's heart was racing. *What's going on?*

"Looks like some kind of ... bird," came the voice over the communicator.

"Nothing on scanners," muttered Captain Tex, checking a handheld device.

There was a gust of wind. Then something dropped from the sky, landing on a nearby tree branch. At once, red laser sights danced across the creature.

Harry frowned. It *was* a bird, with a dark curved beak and black feathers. But

there was something not right about it.
It moved with quick, efficient twitches,
whirring faintly. *It's a robot*, he realised.

A cold feeling settled in his stomach.

"Found you," said the bird. "At last."

The voice was horribly familiar.
Then the bird opened its beak and
light streamed out of it, projecting a
hologram into the clearing below.

Ava gasped softly, and Admiral Achebe
let out an oath. Harry felt the blood
drain from his face.

Vellis.

The hologram flickered in the half-
light. It showed a man dressed in a bulky
body-suit, with robotic enhancements
to support his limbs. A helmet encased

his bald head, the visor raised to reveal tubes going up his nose.

He looked strangely sick. His face was hollow, the skin pale and papery and covered in lesions. Clumps of his short beard had fallen out, leaving it wispy and thin.

But his eyes still glittered fiercely with arrogance and contempt.

The man who betrayed my parents.

Marines had materialised from among the trees, aiming their rifles at the image of Vellis. Admiral Achebe's hand was still raised, holding them in check.

"How does it feel to be home, Harry?" asked Vellis, smirking straight at him.

Harry didn't trust himself to reply.

"Don't worry," snapped Ava. "We're not staying long."

"Is that so?" The scientist's eyebrows raised mockingly. "You know, Harry, I have some friends that you might like to talk to ..."

Vellis held out a hand, and the beam of light widened to show more of the hologram.

Two captives sat in a corner of the room Vellis stood in. They were huddled together, gagged and tied with glowing green energy bonds at their wrists and ankles. One was a slender, pale woman with short dark hair and green eyes. The other was a man, big and broad, with a crooked nose and a shock of silver-blond hair.

Harry's breath caught in his throat. He stumbled forward, until Ava had to hold him back. "It's OK, Harry," she whispered. "It's OK."

But it wasn't. His heart was hammering, and his head was spinning. *Am I dreaming ... is this a nightmare?*

"Mum," he croaked. "Dad."

He had seen them a thousand times in the old holographs he kept on rotation in his quarters. Their faces were a little more lined, their hair shot through with grey, but he would have known them anywhere. And it was only now that he realised the truth – that he had never really, truly believed they were still alive.

But they are.

They couldn't speak with the gags on, but Harry saw how they looked at him, their eyes wide and moist. He felt the tears pricking at his own eyes, wanting so badly to hug them – to hold them and never let go.

"Ahh, how touching," sneered Vellis. "A family reunion … of sorts."

"What do you want?" growled Admiral Achebe.

"And a good evening to you too, Admiral," said Vellis. "Down to business, is it? Very well. I am currently on Gwildor, Avantia's moon. Or at least it was, until the Void knocked it off orbit. I'm carrying out a little … project. Unfortunately, my helpers here are not being very helpful." He turned his glittering gaze on Harry. "And I thought that perhaps they might be persuaded, now they see the alternative …" His smile turned into a scowl. "Which is to watch their only son die."

Harry's heart ached as he saw his parents squirming, trying to slip free and cry out to him. But the energy bonds held firm.

"Don't help him," he told them, unsteadily. "I'm in no danger. And I'm going to rescue you, I prom—"

Vellis snapped his fingers, and the hologram shrank. Harry's parents were gone in an instant.

"No!" gasped Harry.

"Lying to your mother and father, Harry?" said Vellis. He tutted. "I thought better of you. I'm afraid you're not going to rescue them. And you *are* in danger. Very grave danger indeed." He leaned closer and hissed two last words. "*Look up.*"

The hologram flickered, then was

gone. A branch rustled as the bird-droid
took flight.

Slowly, dreading what he might see,
Harry stared up into the darkening sky.

A shadow was descending. A patch of
night with eight flailing limbs that glinted
in the starlight.

10

THE SPIDER AND THE FLY

"Omega Squad! Deploy for combat!" Admiral Achebe already had a phase pistol in her hand, eyes glued to the monster falling from the sky.

"Alpha Team, on me! Beta Team, to the *Intrepid*!" Captain Tex darted into the trees, phase rifle shouldered. Half the marines went with him, scattering to take up defensive positions. They lay flat on the ground, crouched among bushes or hid behind trees.

The remaining marines ran up the access ramp into the ship, boots clanging and pounding the metal.

A sickening *THUD* made the forest floor tremble. The spider had landed, maybe a kilometre away, hidden by trees.

"Go with them," Admiral Achebe hissed at Harry and Ava.

"Let us stay," Harry begged. "Please … I've fought Vellis's robots bef—"

"Enough!" snapped Admiral Achebe. "Huang! Volkova!"

Harry found himself grabbed roughly

from behind and hauled away by one of the marines. He saw Ava struggling in the grip of another, but it was no use. They were forced up the ramp and into the belly of the ruined spacecraft.

Inside, the marines had taken up position along the side of the craft closest to where the spider had landed. Some had opened ports to poke their rifles through, while others had taken seats at the cruiser's gun pods.

Before her marine could stop her, Ava had slipped free and taken one of the gun pods, gripping the handles and engaging the targeting array.

"Stand down!" growled the soldier. "You can't handle that."

Ava gave her a withering glare. "I'm a cadet, thank you very much. And I figure we need all hands on deck right now."

The marine grunted, a glimmer of respect in her eyes. "Just don't get yourself killed, or the Admiral will have my stripes."

Harry looked around, but all the gun pods were taken. There were no spare rifles either. *What am I supposed to do, just sit and watch?* He leaned back against a crate labelled "solar reflectors".

"Don't touch that!" yelled another marine, and Harry bounced back to his feet. He had never felt so useless before. He picked his way through the wrecked ship to the main viewing screen and peered out over the forest below.

At first he couldn't see much. Just skeletal tree branches, moving slightly in the breeze. Everything seemed peaceful.

Then he heard it – the stomping steps of the spider coming closer. He thought he saw it for just a moment, a vast shadow flitting between the trees, but he couldn't be sure …

The forest erupted. Tracer fire arced through darkness, and Harry saw the marines of Alpha Team spread out around the robot. The streaks of their shots lit up the spider, bathing its metal body in a red glow. He heard shouting and saw soldiers scurrying for a better view of the target.

"Hold fire," said a marine with a lieutenant's badge on board the ship.

Harry peered harder at the scene below. He could see phase bolts glancing off the body of the spider, sparking and smoking, but leaving not a single mark.

They can't damage it at all!

The spider's eight eyes glowed like red coals in the darkness, brighter and brighter, and then …

Ffffzzzaaap!

All through the ship, marines gasped and muttered. Harry stared in horror.

The spider was shooting deadly red laser beams from its eyes. They seared through the forest, smashing down trees and setting fires that licked up, coughing smoke into the night.

The marines were falling back now, still firing, phase bolts pattering harmlessly against the spider's metal carapace.

The robot's eyes glowed suddenly brighter, and Harry realised with a lurch what was about to happen. "It's looking at us," he croaked. "It's going to—"

Ffffzzzzaapp! The whole ship shuddered as a burst of laser beams smashed into the hull.

"Fire!" roared the Lieutenant.

The ship rocked again as its blue energy bolts thundered down into the forest. Harry saw Ava, teeth gritted, face glowing blue as she let fly, swivelling in her seat as she strafed left and right.

The forest was a mass of fire and smoke and flashing bolts now. It was impossible to make out the spider.

I've got to do something!

Everyone's attention was fixed on the forest below. No one tried to stop Harry as he charged across the deck and down the ramp, into the cool night air.

He dodged past Admiral Achebe, who was crouching behind a tree trunk and co-ordinating the attack over her communicator. He ran on into the forest, towards where he had seen the Alpha Team. Smoke filled the air, stinging his eyes and making him splutter. His ears rang with the soft *whumph* of phase bolts, the sizzle of the spider's lasers and the heavy thump of its feet.

But he kept running.

"What are you doing? Get back!"

Through the haze of smoke, Harry made out the figure of Captain Tex kneeling behind a fallen tree. His face was bleeding, and his shoulder armour was half melted and scorched black.

Harry was about to run on when he had an idea. He tapped a couple of commands on his prosthetic arm. "Look after your squad," he told Captain Tex. "You don't need to worry about me."

Captain Tex's eyes bulged with fury. "Just who do you think you are?"

Harry's Space Stallion came screaming out of the smoke, skidding to a halt at his side. "Mount up, partner."

Leaping on to the bike, Harry leaned low over the handlebars and tore off, deeper into the forest.

He narrowed his eyes, trying to peer through the smoke that hung all around. Was that a glimpse of a flashing red eye?

WHUMPH! He wobbled, nearly falling

off the Stallion. Something had covered his robotic arm. A thick gloop, like honey but light blue in colour. Underneath it, he saw the LEDs winking out, all at once. *Circuits shorted.*

The blue substance stretched out from his arm into a thick, sticky rope that disappeared up ahead.

Uh oh ... Spider silk.

With a sharp tug he fell hard on to the bumpy ground. He tried to stand, but he was pulled over at once and dragged across the forest floor. He scrabbled hopelessly with his one free hand and his feet, but he couldn't get a grip.

Fear flashed through him.

The spider was reeling him in like a fly.

11

CENTRAL PROCESSING UNIT

Harry bounced and jolted across the ground.

There it was, appearing through the smoke ... Harry's heart stopped as he saw the monster up close for the very first time.

It was even bigger than it had seemed before, each segmented leg twice the height of a fully grown man. Its feet were glinting metal blades that gouged the ground like scythes. Its body was smooth and bulbous with a dull purple sheen, scarred by the phase bolts.

The spider uncurled its abdomen as Harry came to rest in its shadow. Robotics whined faintly as its legs flexed, and its body lowered ominously. Its red eyes were dazzlingly bright, but Harry could see its mouth below, gaping wide, metal jaws opening to crush him …

He tugged desperately, but his arm was completely ensnared.

No time to think. Reaching over with his good arm, Harry flipped open the housing of his prosthetic and jerked at the emergency release.

He fell back at once as the robotic arm catapulted up into the spider's mouth. The jaws clamped shut with a sickening *crunch* and a spray of twisted metal, sparks and shattered diodes. The fingers of the hand twitched grotesquely as the spider began to chew it up.

Harry

didn't stay to watch. He scrambled away into the trees, letting the smoke swallow him. There was no way he could get out of range of the spider's webbing or its laser eyes. *But if it can't see me, I might have a chance.*

Casting around, he spotted a tree with low-hanging branches. His one arm strained to take the weight as he heaved himself up and on to a branch. He settled for a moment, panting. *I'll build another arm*, he told himself. *A better arm. Just need to get through this alive first …*

The tree shuddered with the impact of the spider's stomping feet. It was coming closer.

Harry pulled himself up to a higher

branch and shinned along it, hugging it tightly so he wouldn't fall. He was just reaching for the button to summon his Space Stallion when he realised that it was on the arm he didn't have any more. Lost in the belly of the spider.

He froze. He could see the spider below him, picking its way carefully through the trees. Distant shouts from the marines drifted up to him. *They're retreating*, Harry realised. *Falling back to the safety of the* Intrepid.

He watched, silent, as the robot stalked right below his branch. *It's got to have a weak spot!* He looked all over its smooth, metallic body. There were joints on the legs, and where the legs met the body. But apart from that ...

Wait.

On the rear of its head, Harry spotted the outline of a square hatch. His heart beat faster. *That has to be where its CPU is located – the robotic brain.*

If he could get into that hatch, there was a chance he could disable the spider.

He gulped. *Here goes nothing.*

Swinging his body, Harry dropped on to the spider's back.

He stumbled as he fell, boots skidding on the slippery surface of its body. The spider reared and bucked, but Harry dropped flat on his stomach, squeezing his legs to grip on as best he could.

His fingers found the edge of the

carapace at the spider's neck. Using all his strength, he pulled himself towards the robot's head. The muscles in his one remaining arm burned. He couldn't see any controls to open the head hatch, and he didn't have any of the fancy gadgets built into his prosthetic. So instead he spun round and stomped hard with his boot.

The spider let out an electronic howl of fury. Harry ignored it, stomping again and again. He could feel the metal starting to give. Then … *Yes!* The hatch buckled, revealing an array of blinking lights and circuitry below.

He was reaching into the hatch when he caught sight of the spider's forelegs. They were rotating, twisting in on themselves so that the deadly blades were pointing straight at him …

Harry flung himself to one side, feeling a rush of wind as a blade came slicing at him.

Missed me!

But he was slipping now, sliding off the spider's head. He landed on the ground with a thump, pain stabbing through his ankle as it twisted.

No! There was no way he could see to climb back up, and besides, the second blade was whirring round towards him. The blade glinted in the starlight as it rose to come stabbing down and—

Whooosh!

Something hurtled from the trees. A familiar streak of red and silver, darting right past Harry. Acting on pure instinct, he reached out. His fingers closed over a rubber handlebar. Then his arm was nearly yanked out of its socket as he was dragged along after the Space Stallion.

"Found you, partner," said the Stallion, as Harry swung his leg over and settled in the saddle.

"Much obliged." Harry glanced back, but the spider was already out of view, hidden by the forest.

Up ahead, a distant rumble sounded and beams of red light filtered through the trees. *Must be the* Intrepid*'s engines.* Harry twisted the throttle, speeding faster through the forest.

The access ramp was slowly closing as Harry came roaring out of the trees beside the battle cruiser. He saw Ava standing inside, gesturing wildly at him.

"Get in!"

He leaned a hard left, just squeezing through the narrowing gap before the ramp clunked shut.

The Space Stallion purred to a halt and Harry stepped down on to the deck.

"What happened to your arm?" Ava was staring at him, horrified.

"Never mind that," Harry panted. "I nearly got it! There's this hatch on its head, with the CPU inside, and—"

"Strap in!" Admiral Achebe's voice

came booming over the ship's intercom.

Harry and Ava dashed over to a row of crash seats where the marines were already fastening their flight harnesses. They looked grim, their armour dented, camouflage paint smeared with sweat. But he counted twelve – all alive, at least.

The engine's rumble rose to a roar, deafeningly loud. Viewscreens flickered into life, showing images of the forest outside. *No sign of the spider.*

Harry hoped he really had managed to fix the fuel cells. *If not, we're toast.*

The ship juddered as it left the ground. On the screens, he watched the trees receding. The craft was fifty metres up now, looking down on the shadowy forest as they tore into the night sky.

He hadn't realised he'd been holding his breath. *We made it. We're safe.*

Thump!

The hull shuddered with an impact.

Ava frowned. "What was that?"

"Oh no …" Harry's heart fell as he pointed at the viewscreens. One of them was flickering, the image obscured by a thick blue gloop.

Thump! The vessel shook once again. This time Harry saw the rope of webbing shooting from below, sticking fast to the ship's underside.

"It's trying to pull us back down!" shouted Harry. All around, the marines were wide-eyed with alarm.

Achebe spoke over the intercom.
"Stand by. Engines to maximum."

The ship began to rumble again, worse
than ever.

Harry saw another sticky strand of
webbing fly towards them, snagging
a wing. The whole ship tipped to one
side, and the crate of solar reflectors slid
across the deck to smash into the wall.

"I said, maximum!" Even the Admiral's
voice was panicked now.

Harry didn't hear the pilot's reply, but
he knew the truth. *The fuel cells aren't
up to it*.

And now, slowly but surely, he could
feel the *Intrepid* sinking down again
towards Vellis's monstrous spider.

CHAPTER 12

PROGRAMMED TO DESTROY

"Open fire!" roared Admiral Achebe.
"Blast it to pieces!"

"Negative," grunted Captain Tex.
"Can't get a lock."

Unfortunately, Harry knew he was right. *It's right under us. The cannons don't rotate that far.*

The ship jolted again, sinking lower still.

"What now?" hissed Ava.

Harry's mind was racing, but he was coming up with nothing. *Our blasters barely scratched it. Its lasers are way more powerful.*

Harry frowned as his eyes fell on the crate again. He pointed.

"Hey, Captain Tex. Those reflect the sun's rays, right?'

Tex stared at him, wide-eyed with disbelief. "Great job, kid. You can read."

Harry unclipped his flight harness. The ship jerked again, making him stumble. On the viewscreen he could see the treetops, much closer now, and a flash of dull purple metal as the spider scuttled below.

Harry opened the crate and took out one of the reflectors. It instantly unfolded like a pop-up tent until it was a flat hexagon, about an arm-span wide. It was made of some hi-tech material, shimmering silver. Ships used them when they passed close to stars.

"Captain?" said Harry. "I'll need some cover when we land."

"Are you serious?" growled Tex.

"Do it," snapped Ava. "We're going down whether we like it or not!"

The marines didn't wait for orders. All around, they were unstrapping and manning the gun pods, flicking switches and bringing the energy cannons online.

"I hope you know what you're doing," whispered Ava.

The ship groaned as it hit the ground. Harry clutched the reflector tighter, his heart beginning to pound. *Here goes …*

He darted to a service port. With a yank of the lever, the door slid smoothly open.

"Fire!" yelled Captain Tex behind him.

Harry's ears filled with the thunder of blasting cannons. The forest flared blue with their flashing bolts. He dropped through the port and landed in a crouch on the forest floor.

The Spider was picking its way

through the undergrowth towards the *Intrepid*, bolts sparking off its impenetrable metal body.

"Hey!" he shouted. "Over here!"

The spider froze. Its head swivelled. Its eyes flashed dazzling red.

Then it began to move again, legs jerking up and down, scuttling faster than ever … straight at Harry.

Ignoring his every instinct, Harry stood his ground. He propped the solar reflector against his knees, so that only his torso was visible above it. He angled the reflector carefully. "Come on, robo-bug!" he shouted.

The spider's eyes glowed brighter. Triumph surged through Harry, followed

quickly by fear. *It's working …*

He ducked down behind the reflector.

Ffffzzzaaap!

The reflector slammed into Harry like a fist, knocking him off his feet. He scrambled back, his one good arm aching from the impact. But when he peered over the top of it, his heart leapt.

Yes!

The spider was stumbling, its blade-feet scrabbling at the ground. Smoke poured from its flank, and Harry saw that two of its legs had been sliced clean off. *It's been hit by its own laser!* The beam had reflected straight back at the monster. And unlike the marines' energy cannons, it had done some serious damage.

"That all you got?" Harry yelled.

The spider's head swivelled towards him again, eyes glowing bright.

For a moment Harry thought that he had got it wrong. *How smart is it, really?* He was betting that Vellis had programmed the spider simply to destroy. *But if it figures out what I'm doing …*

Then he heard the faint hum as the lasers charged to fire again. He ducked a second time.

Ffffzzzaaap!

This one knocked him sprawling. His ribs ached – from the fall or the impact of the laser, he couldn't tell. With an effort, he pushed himself up on to his knees. He saw the reflector lying on the ground nearby, charred black and smoking, the shimmering silver material blasted to shreds. *Useless.*

Beyond, the spider had collapsed on to the ground. It was jerking in awkward circles, three more of its legs severed. It flailed wildly, but with only three legs left, it couldn't stand.

The spider was damaged, but not destroyed. Harry saw it lock eyes on him once again. Then its abdomen slowly curled, and he realised with a cold shock what was about to happen. *No shield. No weapon.* It was going to trap him with its webbing. *Then it's going to reel me in and chew me up.*

Harry tensed, ready to dodge aside … when a figure tumbled from the open port of the *Intrepid*.

Ava was sprinting straight for the spider, a phase rifle bouncing on her back.

The robotic monster hesitated, as

if torn between the two targets. It froze just long enough for Ava to duck behind it, shoulder her phase rifle and pull the trigger.

Whumph! The first phase bolt slammed into the back of the spider's head, sending up a spray of sparks. *Whumph! Whumph!* Ava kept firing, over and over.

She's going to destroy its CPU!

The spider twitched and jerked. At the fifth phase bolt, gouts of smoke spilled from its head, and its red eyes went suddenly dull.

"Look out!" yelled Harry.

CRASH!

Ava danced away, just in time, as the

spider collapsed into a heap of junk metal.

In the sudden silence, Harry could hear his heart pounding in his ears.

All was still. Smoke poured silently from the shattered robot.

It's finished … We did it!

Ava grinned at him. Harry found

himself grinning back.

Captain Tex's face appeared at the service port of the *Intrepid*. His narrowed eyes took in the wreckage of the spider.

He gave a gruff nod.

"Hmm," he said. "Not bad."

"Leaving Avantia's atmosphere now, Ma'am," said the pilot, over the intercom.

Harry's heart lifted as they broke through the last of the buffeting storm clouds into the peaceful blackness of space. His repair to the engines had worked. Sighing with relief, the marines unclipped their harnesses and began to float in zero gravity.

Harry did the same and made his way to the cockpit. Admiral Achebe was sitting in the navigation seat, next to the pilot.

"Set a course—" she was saying.

"For Gwildor!" interrupted Harry.

The Admiral turned and raised an eyebrow. "So now you're giving the orders?"

"Sorry." Harry felt a blush creep across his cheeks. "I only mean … because that's where Vellis is, isn't it? And my parents. And if he's got them, who knows how many other captives he—"

"No," said the Admiral.

Harry gulped. "What do you mean?"

"This is not a rescue ship, Harry," said Admiral Achebe. "We've got no idea what defences Vellis might have on Gwildor. We can't just go charging in there." She spoke softly, calmly, as though she were talking to a little child.

But we children saved your life, Harry thought.

"We defeated that spider." He had raised his voice, but he didn't care. Anger was burning through him. "Ava and I rescued you all! We can take Vellis. I know we can."

"No." The Admiral was stony-faced.

"Then I'll go on my own!"

"You will not."

Harry saw the Admiral looking past

him, giving a nod.

Before he could react, he was grabbed from behind. A marine held him, locking his arm behind his back. Harry struggled, but it was hopeless. He let out a howl of frustration. His eyes were hot with tears. *My parents! He's got my parents ...*

Admiral Achebe wasn't even looking at him any more. "Open a channel to Vantia1," she told the pilot. "Inform Governor Knox that we've got the kids ... and that we're coming home."

Harry was turned and marched back into the belly of the ship

"We going to have any problems?" asked the marine.

Harry just grunted and tugged his arm free. There was no use fighting any more. The Admiral had spoken, and there were a dozen marines on this ship, with orders to keep him here. He flung himself down on a cargo crate, head drooping.

"Harry?"

He looked up to see Ava, her brown eyes full of determination. In spite of everything, it made him feel a little better.

"We'll get them back. I promise." She sat beside him and put an arm around his shoulders. "You didn't give up on my mum. No way am I giving up on yours."

Harry smiled through his tears.

"Thanks," he managed to say.

Ava hesitated. "Mum's right, though," she said at last. "We should do it when we're ready. When we know exactly what we're up against."

Harry was starting to think more clearly now. *Vellis won't hurt them. Not while he needs them for his project.*

He dried his eyes and nodded. "We'll save them, all right. We'll come back here, into the Void. We'll rescue everyone that Vellis has taken."

His one remaining hand clenched into a fist.

And then … Then we'll make him pay.

The End